TERROR AT THE SWEET SHOP

LAWRENCE PRESTIDGE

TERROR AT THE SWEET SHOP

ILLUSTRATED BY

G. WILLIAM

Matador
9 Priory Business Park,
Wistow Road, Kibworth Beauchamp,
Leicestershire. LE8 0RX
Tel: 0116 279 2299
Email: books@troubador.co.uk
Web: www.troubador.co.uk/matador
Twitter: @matadorbooks

ISBN 978 1785899 072

British Library Cataloguing in Publication Data.
A catalogue record for this book is available from the British Library.

Printed by TJ International Ltd, Padstow, Cornwall
Typeset in 11pt Minion Pro by Troubador Publishing Ltd, Leicester, UK

Matador is an imprint of Troubador Publishing Ltd

For My Parents –
Thank You For Everything

"A little nonsense now and then is relished by the wisest man" – Roald Dahl

PROLOGUE

I USED TO LOVE GOING TO the sweet shop after school. At 3:20 every day, my friends and I would congregate at the school gates and march down in a group to the greatest shop in the world. Every time we visited the sweet shop we had to pick what sweets to get, which is the *hardest decision ever.*

During my lifetime, I've had to make some very important decisions, what subjects to study at school, what job to do and who to vote for as prime minister. But I can honestly say, having the responsibility to pick which sweets to have each day was as tough as it gets. Speaking of hard decisions, ranking my top five types of sweets was just as hard.

Apple Bon Bons
Mini Marshmallows
Giant Strawberries
Milk Bottles
Giant Snakes

Going to the sweet shop was one of my favourite things about school life. Now this story begins in a normal sweet shop in a normal town, but I must warn you it is a tale of terror and is not for the faint of heart. What happens when evil takes over your most beloved sweet shop?

1

OSCAR TARRANT WAS A POPULAR BOY at school. He was on the school team for football, rugby and athletics. He had many friends, but he had three especially close ones. His best friend was Reece Goodman, another talented footballer who also spent a lot of time on his BMX. Then there was Ishmaael Kahn (Ishy to his friends) who was a computer geek. You have *never* seen anyone type on a computer quicker than Ishy and you *never* will. Oscar would often watch how fast Ishy typed in pure amazement. Finally there was Emma Baker who loved drama and music. She was in all the school performances. She loved to sing as well as playing *four* different musical instruments. They were:

The Flute

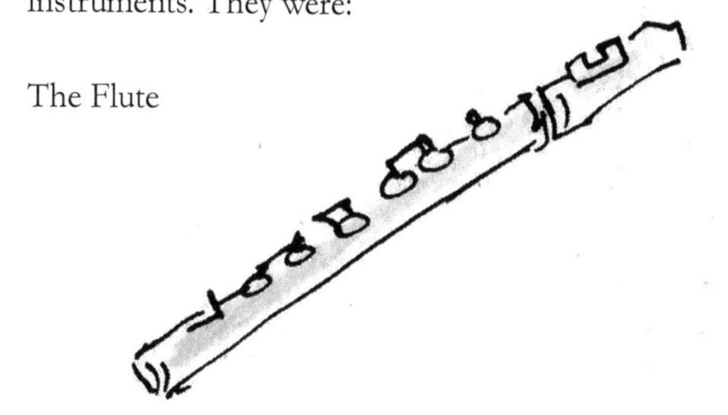

The Piano

The Guitar

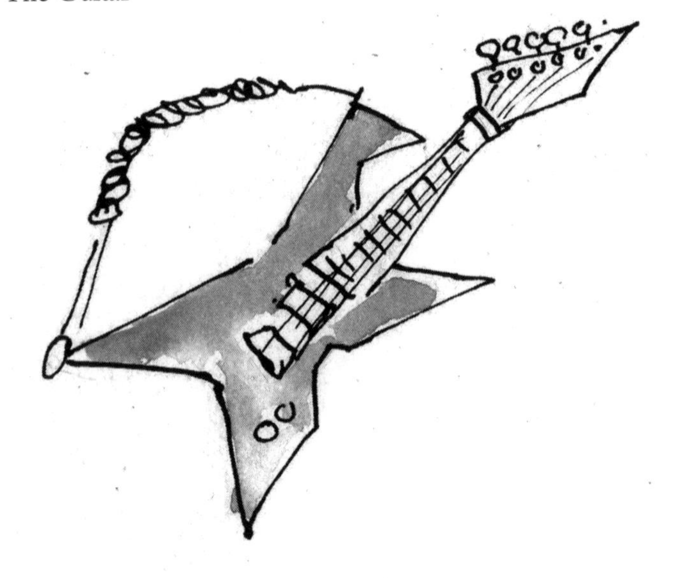

And finally…
The Drums

When her parents got Emma her first drum set, they soon regretted encouraging that one.

The one thing that these four friends all had in common would come at the end of the day when they walked to Mr McNulty's sweet shop.

Mr McNulty was very nice, a jolly-looking man with a red and bulbous nose which made him look like that famous man from the North Pole.

Not once did they walk into his shop and see him angry or upset. He was always friendly. Whether the rain was falling or the sun was shining, Mr.McNulty's friendly smile would always glow. He even insisted Oscar and his friends call him Mick which meant, "He must like us!" according to Ishy.

They hardly ever did call him that, but Mr McNulty said that was fine as well.

The one thing the friends couldn't help noticing about Mr McNulty was the ridiculous-looking toupee on the top of his head. It wasn't even a convincing one. It looked as though someone had run over a small animal – very slowly – several times, and then for some strange reason decided to place it on the top of Mr McNulty's head.

"Don't stare!" Emma would often whisper to the boys, but they couldn't help it, the girls couldn't help it either but they were way more subtle at looking than the boys.

The highlight of any school child's day was walking up to Mr McNulty's shop after school. When you walked in and saw all the different jars behind him at the counter it was like the pearly gates of heaven.

Only five children were allowed to be in the shop at a time because of a boy called Dan Rosamound. You see he kept swiping sweets and scoffing his face in the shop whenever it was really busy and poor old Mr McNulty didn't see how much Dan was devouring until it was too late.

Rumour has it he exploded…

But anyway, since then, there has always been a great long line waiting to get into the sweet shop every day after school. It was certainly worth the wait.

Oscar normally had the same routine every day after school. He would go for the toffee bon-bons. His mum always insisted he got his love of toffees from his granddad, a man who after losing his teeth at the age of

73, was able to make a single toffee last a whole day! He used to keep it in his hanky at mealtimes. He loved toffees more than Christmas!

Reece was a rebel who seemed to mix up his selection every day. He was always the most experimental of the group when it came to trying out different sweets.

Ishy would go for the giant snakes – always explaining to the poor thing why he would be eating it before viciously biting its head off.

For Emma it was fizzy cola bottles or fried eggs – it was a running joke in the group which one she would go for that day. One time though, she got some strawberry laces – a very controversial move!

The visit to Mr McNulty's sweet shop was a daily ritual for the group, as it was for most of the children at the school. So you can imagine how horrified they were when there were some nasty changes at their favourite shop which was named 'McNulty's Candy Kingdom'.

2

THE SHOP WAS ALWAYS CLOSED ON a Monday, which made Mondays even more unbearable than usual. When Tuesdays came along, you could taste the excitement in the air round school – but this Tuesday would be different – and not in a good way!

The sun was out as Oscar and his friends walked towards the sweet shop from school.

"What sweets are you thinking of today, Reece?" Oscar asked.

"I think I've got a craving for jelly hearts with a hint of bubblegum-flavoured bon-bon on the side," Reece joked. "Oh, and the liquorice laces! They're lush," he added.

As the group approached the sweet shop there was an unfamiliar commotion outside of it. And where was Tuesday's line of eager customers?

Oscar looked over to a group of the older boys as he tried to eavesdrop on what was being said.

"McNulty's gone!" one of the boys cried out in disgust as he left the shop.

"I bet she's done him in!" another shouted. "You

should see what that woman has done to the shop! Not a giant strawberry in sight!"

"What a rotten woman," a girl muttered as she walked out. "I do hope Mr McNulty comes back soon."

Oscar felt more than a bit concerned. He and his friends anxiously approached the shop and were able to walk straight in without waiting. Oscar couldn't believe how much the shop had changed since Friday. The same shop that was once a ray of light after a long school day had transformed into a dark and gloomy place.

"What's happened?" Emma asked.

"Is this even the right shop?" Reece asked, puzzled.

The friends looked behind the counter and were horrified by what they saw. There stood a tall, pale woman wrapped in black. She wore a long black dress and her lank, lifeless hair hung down on her stooped shoulders. As for her face? Now that was gruesome. She had feline-like eyes that shimmered with hatred; a hooked and misshapen nose, underneath which were teeth that looked like pieces of broken glass. According to her dusty name badge, her name was Miss Primrose.

On the very top shelf nestled in a corner was a unfamiliar black cat. It stared down at the children and seemed to be watching them like a hawk.

"Hello poppets," the woman called out in a hissing wheezy tone. "I am Miss Primrose. How can I help you?"

"Oh hi…where's Mr McNulty?" Oscar asked, as politely as he could.

Miss Primrose almost seemed disgusted by the question, this clearly wasn't the first time she'd been asked that question today and she'd had enough.

"He's gone away. I'm in charge now." She smirked, showing her razor teeth.

"When will he be back?" asked Ishy.

"Who knows, my sweet…I'm not too sure," she answered.

Mikey Phillips waddled into the shop. He was Oscar's age and was known as being the fattest kid in his class. He didn't particularly smell nice either, if you were around Mikey too long you couldn't help but notice the stink of strong onions. Mikey thought it was normal for people to walk around covering their nose and mouth because that's what people did whenever they were around him, even the teachers! Mikey hated to shower or bath because it stopped him from eating sweets, he did once try eating a sherbet dip in the bath but it went badly and now Mikey refuses to even think about cleanliness.

He came and stood next to Oscar, examining the jars of sweets behind the counter.

The jars had been changed and the sweets inside looked completely different. Mikey didn't really care, he loved all sweets and was happy to try anything new whenever he could. The strange thing was though that one of them looked like a jar full of live worms!

"Are these real worms?" Mikey asked curiously.

Miss Primrose leaned back and laughed. "Of course not dearie," she cackled. "They are made completely of liquorice! Liquorice worms as a matter of fact! They're new. You should try them. Trust me, they are delicious."

"I'll have one bag please!" Mikey slammed a shiny fifty pence piece on the counter.

Miss Primrose's eyes sparkled and a devilish grin appeared on her face.

Oscar sensed something wasn't right about the situation. The tension filled the shop like hot steam.

Miss Primrose scooped some of the 'liquorice worms' into a bag and handed them to Mikey.

Mikey looked into the bag. "Wow! They look really realistic!" he cried in excitement.

Oscar wanted to warn Mikey that something wasn't right. "Mikey, I wouldn't do–"

"*Shut up you little brat!*" screamed Miss Primrose before composing herself. "I mean, why don't you be a dear and let Mikey enjoy his sweeties in peace?"

Mikey picked out a handful of those worms and looked at them with excitement. Oscar was sure he saw one move but Mikey wasn't paying attention, he opened his fat fingers and gulped those worms into his greedy gob. The sight was unpleasant to say the least – actually the sight was worse than that, far worse. It was royally repulsive, repugnant and retch inducing. Oscar's stomach knotted, twisted and lurched into his throat, Mikey just looked confused.

"Well?" Miss Primrose asked as she rubbed her grimy hands together.

"They don't really taste of anything," said Mikey disappointedly. "I couldn't taste any liquorice at all; they just tasted slimy."

Oscar and his friends started to fear the worst.

"Do you want to know why that is?" Miss Primrose sniggered.

"Sure," replied Mikey.

"*Because they were real worms*!" Miss Primrose shouted and she bellowed with laughter.

Oscar and his friends looked at each other in horror and disgust. Mikey on the other hand began to turn a very odd shade of green.

"Mikey, are you okay?" Oscar asked.

The shop went silent as all eyes were focused on Mikey. He got greener and greener.

"He's turning into the Hulk!" Ishy cried, as Miss Primrose continued to cry out with laughter.

Then the inevitable happened.

After turning the most bizarre shade of green you have ever seen, Mikey was sick all over the sweet shop floor. It seemed he was puking up everything he had ever eaten. It was like a vomit tsunami hit the shop. Reece even swore he saw Mikey puke out half a tennis ball.

Mikey had now gone from Incredible Hulk green to ghostly white. Then, like a tower of jelly, he began to wobble from side to side.

"*Timber*!" shouted Ishy as Mikey, like a great tree that had been cut down in the forest, began to slowly plummet. It was like stacking up loads of tin cans and seeing it begin to shake. Just as the tower begins to fall, everybody sees it coming. Mikey fainted and unfortunately as he landed, he was bathed in a pool of his own vomit. The gang had to dodge the tidal waves of puke on the shop floor

"Why would you do that?" Oscar shouted at Miss Primrose. "What did Mikey ever do to you?"

Miss Primrose sniggered at Oscar and his friends before replying. "Let's get one thing straight, you little beasts! The problem with children these days is they are always getting their own way. It's always *me, me, me* or *my, my, my* or *now, now, now*. They think they are so clever but they're not. I see right through you all. Do you understand what I am saying to you? Children are vermin and like vermin they should be exterminated. I promise you sticky-fingered little brats I'm going to make sure every child that enters my shop gets *exactly* what they deserve. That's my job – to destroy you. I shall destroy you and then feed you to the termites and then crush the termites till there is *nothing left*! All you children are disgusting! Now, unless you are willing to purchase some goodies yourself I suggest you get out of my shop!"

Oscar and his friends didn't need to be told twice. They ran from the shop and into the street.

"I really hope Mr McNulty comes back soon. Poor Mikey," sighed Emma.

"But what if he doesn't?" Oscar said in fear. "What if Mr McNulty never comes back?"

"*Don't talk like that!*" cried out Ishy.

"Why wouldn't he come back?" Reece questioned.

"I don't know. But there's something strange going on and you can bet we're going to find out exactly what it is," Oscar said confidently.

3

OSCAR AND HIS FRIENDS WERE IN his bedroom still coming to terms with what they had witnessed at the sweet shop.

"I do hope Mikey's all right," Emma sighed.

"Poor Mikey?! What about my new trainers!"cried Reece "covered in sick!"

"We need to forget about it. What can we do to make sure this never happens to anyone again?" asked Oscar.

"Can't we just wait till Mr McNulty comes back?" Ishy suggested.

"That's just it though Ish, what if Mr McNulty is *never* coming back?" Oscar said firmly. The room suddenly went silent. "There is something about Miss Primrose that isn't right. I'm worried she has Mr McNulty locked up somewhere as a prisoner."

"We don't know that though, he could be on holiday," Reece pointed out.

"Didn't you see how strange she got when we asked where Mr McNulty was?" said Oscar.

"He has a point," Emma agreed. "She said she was going to make sure every child gets exactly what they deserve. I mean what if she serves every kid bags full of worms or something even worse?"

"That's exactly it, Emma," Oscar said. "What if it does get worse?"

"What do you mean?" asked Reece.

"Well today it's the sweet shop. What if she starts to take over more and more of our favourite places? Imagine if she became a playground assistant and took over our playground. Imagine if she started putting worms in the food at the canteen!"

"Don't say such a thing!" squeaked Ishy in horror.

"It could happen though, Ishy. You heard what she said. She said she thought all kids should be exterminated," Oscar reminded him.

"I can't help worrying about some of the other things Miss Primrose said. Why does she think kids are so bad and horrible?" wondered Emma.

"It's not us that's horrible – we're living in horrible times. When my parents watch the news I see such horrible things. I don't think the grown-ups always get it right, personally," stated Ishy.

"Ishy's right," said Oscar. "When we grow up we're going to stick together and be good adults in a good world, looking out for each other. When I grow up I'll be tall enough to ride any rollercoaster in the world and I'll ride on one every day! I'll get my own rollercoaster then everyone can just ride on it for free!"

"When I grow up I'll lift all the weights those strong guys do at the gym," chimed in Ishy. "I will help carry the old ladies across the street and be able to help Mum carry the shopping with my muscles!"

"I'll be eating sweets and ice cream every day," said Reece.

"Staying up late every night and watching the stars." Emma smiled.

"We'll get to play football at the park all the time," said Oscar hopefully.

"I can't wait!" said Ishy. "When we're adults we are *so* doing it right."

"But Miss Primrose is the worst kind of grown up," Emma groaned. "How do we stop her?"

"I've got a plan – but you guys should probably know if we get caught we could get in some real trouble. Or even worse…get grounded!" Oscar warned.

"It's a risk we're going to have to take," Reece said heroically.

"Yeah. I mean, what if Spider Man never stood up to the Green Goblin?" Ishy agreed.

"What if Wayne Rooney didn't take that penalty for England?" Oscar added.

"What if Harry Potter said, 'you know what? I don't really fancy Hogwarts'," said Reece.

"What if Snow White was never kissed by Prince Charming?" Emma said with a smile.

"Errrr…Sure, imagine that." Ishy raised an eyebrow.

"Guys, tomorrow we are going to create our own story by saving our sweet shop and finding out where Mr McNulty is. We'll save him. Every kid everywhere will remember our bravery. We will go down in history as official…legends. Who's with me?" Oscar reached out his hand.

"Count me in," Ishy instantly put his hand on top of Oscar's.

"Me too," added Reece as he reached his hand out.

"I suppose you guys will need a girl's brain to help

you out." Emma sighed as she put her hand on the top of the pile.

"Sometimes us kids have to create a bit of trouble," Oscar said with a wink.

4

THE NEXT DAY THE GANG HAD come up with a plan and how they would put it into action.

"Stink her out?" Ishy asked, puzzled.

"That's right. If we could make it smell so bad in the sweet shop she had to leave – that'll give us time to get rid of her for a while and find Mr McNulty!" Oscar explained.

"So how are we going to 'stink her out' exactly?" questioned Emma.

Oscar looked at Reece and nodded as Reece began to unzip his bag.

"TA-DA! The REEKFEST 4000," Reece presented proudly. "Me and Oscar put some of our pocket money together and got it last night!"

"It's actually real..." Ishy said in amazement.

"What do you mean by the REEKFEST 4000?" Emma asked.

"Emma, all joking aside, this is the stickiest, smelliest, most disgusting stink bomb in the world," explained Oscar.

"Most countries have banned it," added Reece.

"It's beautiful!" Ishy said with a tear in his eye.

"That's how you expect us to get rid of Miss Primrose! A stupid stink bomb!" Emma groaned.

The boys all gasped

"Don't call it stupid, Emma…it might hear you," Ishy warned in a whisper.

"*Hear me*?"

"Never underestimate the power of the REEKFEST 4000," intoned Reece.

"Oh really? Why's that?"

"I heard at one school; they used it on a supply teacher and the smell was *so* revolting the teacher had to cut off his nose to get rid of the rancid smell" said Oscar.

"I heard some kids threw one into the school's staff room and that when the smell finally cleared all the teachers had disappeared, and were *never* seen again," Reece added.

"That's nothing!" shouted Ishy as he braced himself to tell a more tragic story. "I heard one time this kid was going to let one off as a joke in a big store over the Christmas period, but something terrible happened. He was in the lift with his friends heading to the ladies' gift floor, laughing about the terror he was about to unleash when: he dropped it."

Oscar and Reece gasped but Emma raised her eyebrow in suspicion as Ishy went on, "They tried their best to catch it, but it was too late. The REEKFEST 4000 exploded. They never did find the kid and his friends, all that was left was a pool of foul smelling slime on the bottom of the lift. Those kids were literally melted by the smell."

"What a way to go," Reece sighed.

"Dare I ask where all three of you heard these stories?" Emma questioned and all three boys answered in unison, "The Internet".

"I say no more," said Emma as she rolled her eyes.

The three boys could tell Emma was not impressed with these stories. They looked at each other, unsure what else to say before Reece repeated, "Never underestimate the power of the REEKFEST 4000".

"Besides, I've got a plan on top of a plan," Oscar bragged.

"And that is?" Emma asked.

"Mikey Phillips of course."

"Go on…" Emma said more keenly.

"Well we all know Mikey will want to get his revenge on Miss Primrose, right?" said Oscar.

"Right," muttered Reece.

"And who do we know that does the most vile, disgusting farts in class?" asked Oscar.

"Mikey! Of course!" cried Ishy.

"Exactly – so with the REEKFEST 4000 and Mikey Phillips dropping power farts at the same time, there is no way Miss Primrose will be able to be in that shop for days!" explained Oscar.

Emma was more accepting of this idea. She had seen…well…smelt a Mikey Phillips' fart first hand and it certainly was traumatic.

"Imagine what a stink bomb *and* a Mikey Phillips' fart could do!" Reece said with excitement.

"I've just had an apostrophe!" Ishy yelled.

"I think you mean an epiphany," Emma corrected.

"My dad makes the strongest, spiciest curry at our restaurant. Imagine if we got Mikey to eat that before he farted, as well as using the REEKFEST 4000!!" Ishy suggested.

"Ishy, that's genius!" Oscar said.

"Well… y'know…" Ishy shrugged with a grin.

The next step would be to get Mikey on board and begin to bring Miss Primrose's reign of terror to an abrupt end.

5

"YOU WANT ME TO DO WHAT?" cried Mikey when the group had approached him at school.

"Fart," Ishy said, bluntly.

"We're going to stink her out," Oscar added.

"I don't know, guys. It's a lot of pressure. Especially on my bum. I'm not sure my farts are so bad they'd make her leave anyway," Mikey said hesitantly.

"I'm not so sure about that Mikey," Emma said with a disgusted look.

"Besides, we got you some back-up." Reece pulled the REEKFEST 4000 out of his bag.

"Is that what I think it is?" Mikey gasped.

"That's right. The REEKFEST 4000," Oscar said proudly.

Mikey's mouth was open wide in pure amazement. A swarm of flies could have ventured into it, like an insect caving expedition.

"Can I…touch it?" Mikey asked in a whisper as he reached his hand out.

"No," whispered back Reece as he moved the stink bomb out of Mikey's reach.

"So what do you say, Mikey? Are you in?" Oscar asked.

Mikey was very hesitant. He didn't particularly want to take on Miss Primrose but he, like all the kids at school, *loved* that sweet shop. The thought of losing it was unbearable.

"You will go down in history as a hero," Ishy tried to egg Mikey on.

"A legend," added Emma.

A small smirk suddenly appeared on Mikey's face.

"See, I like the sound of that." Mikey grinned.

"You'll be showered with sweets from thankful kids everywhere you go," said Oscar.

"Are you sure this is going to work?" questioned Mikey.

"Helllooooooo. REEKFEST 4000!" Reece reminded.

In Mikey's head the thought of being a legend was too good to resist. He pictured all the kids in the playground lifting him high in the air as they chanted: "*Mikey, Mikey, Mikey!*" and "*We love you, Mikey!*" and "*Mikey, you are so incredibly handsome and definitely not fat!*"

"Okay. I'm in," Mikey agreed.

6

WHEN ISHY WENT HOME THAT DAY, he had to persuade his dad to make his legendary curry. It wouldn't be hard to convince him. His dad was very proud of his signature dish.

Ishy's parents owned a restaurant called 'Curry Fusion'. It was the most popular restaurant in town; a family-owned business which kept his parents and older sisters working around the clock because it was always so busy.

The dish Ishy wanted was entitled the 'Chicken Tindaloo' and the ingredients were as follows:

CHICKEN
FRESH CHILLIES
LAMB
DRIED HOT CHILLIES
GARLIC
DRIED RED HOT CHILLI PEPPERS
ONION
DRIED MEGA HOT CHILLI PEPPERS
COCONUT
WHITE VINEGAR
MUSTARD POWDER
AND ONE GHOST CHILLI

Ishy had tried a mouthful once and that was enough to give him an upset tummy for a week! It certainly took its toll on anyone who ate it.

Mr Kahn was delighted to prepare one of his dishes for Ishy. He didn't even ask his son why he needed to take it to school, so Ishy didn't need to use the food tech excuse he'd prepared.

Ishy was mesmerised whenever he watched his dad cooking, he was like a magician with food; everything was always timed to perfection. Although this curry was only for the bravest of eaters. Ishy couldn't help admiring the way his dad cooked, he couldn't get over his dad's concentration on the preparation and he could feel his passion for the food.

"That'll be perfect for you tomorrow Ishy. You just need to reheat it at school," Mr Kahn said proudly. "Here, take some of this special hot curry powder. But only use one teaspoon of it. It gives it that extra kick."

When the food was prepared for Ishy to take in the next day, Ishy had a quick look. Even looking at the dish directly was enough to make his eyes water. He did not envy Mikey eating it, not one little bit.

7

THE NEXT DAY WHEN THE bell rang and the gang met after school, it was the moment of truth. Mikey arrived, bright red and sweating buckets; his hands were clammy and he kept blinking due to the sweat running in his eyes. The whole gang was nervous. Their hearts were pounding like drumbeats as soon as the bell rang.

"Are you okay Mikey?" asked Emma.

"Yeah, this happens when I get nervous," Mikey replied.

"Don't worry Mikey, this idea is flawless," reassured Oscar.

"Yeah, don't get so worked up," added Reece.

"It's not just that…I've been holding in that curry ever since lunch when Ishy warmed it up for me! I've been fighting it ever since," Mikey explained.

"Yeah guys, judging by the look of him we shouldn't waste much time. We need to go right now," Ishy insisted.

The group marched to the shop as quickly as they could with Mikey slowly waddling, like a bloated penguin, behind them. They had to move quickly, otherwise Mikey would explode before they even made it to the shop.

The plan was simple: Emma had to distract Miss Primrose at the counter, while Oscar and Reece prepare the REEKFEST 4000, then Ishy had to give Mikey the signal for when to 'let rip'.

The group walked into the shop, their hearts beating like drums due to the nerves.

Miss Primrose snarled at them as they walked in, before sniggering as she spotted Mikey. "Well look who it is!" she cackled. "Come for second helpings have we?"

Miss Primrose approached Mikey slowly. She stared at him intensely; there was something quite hypnotic about her eyes, they could almost send a person into a trance. It looked as though Miss Primrose was about to make an example out of Mikey again but Emma diverted her attention so the boys could set up the plan.

"Miss Primrose, this jar of frog's eyes looks very... interesting. I'd very much love to know what sweets they are made of," Emma said.

Miss Primrose rolled her eyes at the inconvenience before revealing a crooked smile. Another potential victim, she thought as she slithered like a serpent towards Emma and the jar to which she referred. "Well, these sweets are awfully special. Quite a unique taste I must say. You know what, my dear, I will even let you try one *free* of charge to see if you like them," said Miss Primrose as she drew closer and closer to Emma.

She grabbed one of the 'frog's eyes' out of the jar and reached out to Emma. As it drew ever closer to her mouth, everyone was positive that it was a *real* frog's eye.

"Oh no, I couldn't possibly have one for free," said Emma and she slowly backed away, thrusting the frog's eye back towards the grinning Miss Primrose.

"Oh dear child, don't worry; I insist. It's only fair that a sweet little child gets her just desserts," Miss Primrose murmered.

A hiss broke the tension as Miss Primrose's cat leapt forward snatching the eye from her outstretched hand. It seemed that the cat was very keen on frog's eyes!

Oscar knew there was now no more time to spare. They had to act before she grabbed another.

"*Now*," he whispered to Ishy.

Ishy was hoping for more of a dramatic countdown but Mikey could not wait any longer.

"10…9…8…7…" Ishy muttered to Mikey.

"6 5 4 3 2 1!" Mikey called out as quickly as he could before letting rip.

It was the *biggest, smelliest fart* Mikey had ever done. It was the loudest fart any of them had *ever* heard. It was the loudest fart any of them had heard *about!* It was as if the entire world went silent just so that fart might exist.

The foul, disgusting gas that Mikey released swam past Ishy, pushed past Oscar and Reece, and crawled past Emma, that demon fart that seemed to have a mind of its own as it dived into the face of Miss Primrose!

You could almost hear the impact as it landed on

her face. Miss Primrose stumbled a few steps back as it slammed into her.

Silence filled the shop. But Mikey began to feel the aftermath. "Houston…we have a problem," Mikey said in horror.

Yeah, that's right. Mikey had followed through, and although he had delivered the fart the gang knew he was capable of – he certainly didn't do his pants any favours.

Miss Primrose began assessing the fart in the air – she even stuck her tongue out into thin air to taste it. Although she was repulsed by the smell she was determined to track down the culprit.

It didn't take her longer than a few seconds to direct her attention straight at Mikey.

"*You*!" she screamed. "How dare you spread your rotten bowel gas in my shop!"

She was halfway to Mikey before Oscar and Reece yelled, "*Leg it*!"

The gang only had a few seconds, as the REEKFEST 4000 was about to explode. They turned and ran, diving out of the doorway before the shop shook with the exploding rumble of the REEKFEST 4000.

They turned around and saw an oppressive dark-green gas fill the windows and slowly begin to sneak out of the cracks of the windows and doors.

The gang looked on at the shop. Surely Miss Primrose would require nose surgery and a team of experts to eliminate the vulgar stench that would linger there for days. The plan had succeeded. The group were overjoyed...all except Mikey who simply said, "I really need to change my pants!"

8

THE NEXT DAY OSCAR FELT refreshed, like a weight had been lifted from his shoulders. Miss Primrose had been driven from the shop and it wouldn't take long to track down Mr McNulty. Life was good.

As Oscar walked to school, he saw men wearing gas masks entering the shop and no sign of Miss Primrose.

Job done, Oscar thought as he walked past.

To top it off, the only allied casualty was Mikey's pants, this was a good plan that came together. But this feeling of relief, bliss and sheer delight was very short-lived.

As Oscar entered school that day he noticed his year group lined up in military fashion in the playground. As more pupils in his year group got to school that day they were soon directed to join this intimidating-looking formation.

Oscar stood himself next to Emma in the line-up.

"What's going on?" Oscar whispered to Emma.

"Beats me," she replied. "As soon as anyone in our year group got here, teachers were directing them to line up here. You don't think it's to do with 'stinkergate' do you?"

Before Oscar could answer, the playground was forced silent as the head teacher, Mr Fazey, walked into the playground to address them.

Mr Fazey wasn't what you expect your typical head teacher to look like. He certainly saw himself as very rock'n'roll and always tried to be as mellow as possible. It was fair to say he modelled himself on Elvis Presley. He had the big Elvis hair, the Elvis swagger in his walk and he even sported the tight Elvis leather trousers.

It wasn't too scary seeing Mr Fazey approach the year group. He was always very laid back and chilled. What was scary, well actually more like terrifying, was the person walking directly behind him – and that was Miss Primrose.

Mr Fazey and Miss Primrose approached the year group in the playground. Miss Primrose had a dark purple handkerchief that she continuously held to her nose.

"How can she be standing?" Oscar whispered to Emma.

"Maybe the stink bomb wasn't as strong as legend suggests," Emma muttered back.

Mr Fazey had a megaphone in his hand to address the year group. He was extremely softly spoken, so he carried a megaphone everywhere he went. He raised the megaphone and slowly began talking.

"Okay guys, so, I believe there was an incident yesterday at Miss Primrose's sweet shop which has left her shop needing emergency cleansing. This isn't cool guys. I'm hoping rather than Miss Primrose point out the culprit, that person will be honest and come forward and accompany me and Miss Primrose to my office immediately," announced Mr Fazey.

"Culprit?" Emma whispered to Oscar. "Surely he means *culprits*?"

None of the kids in the playground stepped forward to claim responsibility for 'stinkergate' as it was being referred to in the playground.

Mr Fazey sighed. "Very well, I have to say I am very disa–"

Before Mr Fazey could continue with his sentence, Miss Primrose snatched the megaphone from his hand – whilst still holding her handkerchief firmly on her nose with the other hand.

"As far as I'm concerned, you are all *guilty*! All of you liars, all criminals, all villains, all gangsters, all members of the mafia – *all rotten little worms*! But I have to make an example out of one of you. The true culprit, the criminal mastermind that you elected... *you*!" she screamed as she pointed in Oscar's direction.

"You!" she growled as she pushed the megaphone towards Mr Fazey and started to march.

Oscar took a large gulp. He was ready to take responsibility. He was kind of glad the others weren't getting in trouble. After all it was his idea.

"You!" Miss Primrose repeatedly grunted as she stepped closer and closer to Oscar.

Oscar closed his eyes and took a deep breath. He wasn't sure what his punishment would be – but he was certain it was going to be far from pleasant.

Shockingly however, when Oscar opened his eyes, Miss Primrose had marched past both him and Emma. Down the line was Mikey Phillips who was wobbling with fear as Miss Primrose stood directly in front of him.

"Well boy, do you have anything to say?" Miss Primrose asked as she towered above Mikey.

"Well. I uh–" Mikey muttered before being immediately cut off by Miss Primrose.

"Of course you don't have anything to say. Because there is nothing to say is there? Did you really think someone as pathetic as you could out-match me? Of course not. Because you are a child, and children are idiots! Hooligans! So now you boy – yes you – must pay the price. Your vulgar smelling, stinky bottom-belching, bum-bazooking, steam spitting fart *ruined* my stock. The frog's eyes, the rotten fried eggs, the snakes, the shrimps, the sour snails and your personal favourites the worms, have all gone bad! You are going to eat every last one of those sweets you ruined, you hear me boy? Every last frog's eye, every rotten fried egg, every last snake, every shrivelled shrimp, every sour snail and every last worm!

Do you understand me?" Miss Primrose bellowed as she grabbed Mikey and started to drag him in Mr Fazey's direction.

Oscar's blood boiled – he wasn't going to stand for it.

"*You can't do that!*" he yelled. "He'll be sick. We all know what those sweets really are! He'll never want to step inside a sweet shop again!"

"Well he should have thought of that before he made a pact with Satan and decided to fart in my shop!" screamed Miss Primrose as she glared intensely at Oscar. A horrible smirk appeared on her face before she continued dragging Mikey away.

Oscar and Emma watched as Mikey was guided to the head's office.

"What are we going to do?" Emma asked.

"Tonight, we are getting into that sweet shop and looking for whatever clues we can. Miss Primrose is up to something and we are going to find out *exactly* what that is," replied Oscar.

9

THAT NIGHT THE GANG planned to break into the sweet shop, determined to find any shred of information that would reveal what Miss Primrose was up to. Emma insisted they all wore black to blend in with the darkness. There was Emma covered head to toe in black, she even wore black nail varnish. Reece's effort wasn't quite as committed since he turned up in his new luminescent pair of trainers.

"You sure this is a good idea?" muttered Reece as the group stared at the sweet shop.

"Trust me. It's fine," answered Oscar.

"I'm not sure the police would agree," sighed Reece.

"I'm more worried about the smell in there!" Ishy whispered. "This is like suicide!"

"Face it," Emma butted in bluntly. "Although that stink bomb combined with Mikey's revolting fart was rather disgusting – it clearly didn't live up to our expectations; we will be fine."

Reece started to mutter, "Never underestimate the pow–"

"*Shut up*!" Emma snapped.

"Ready guys? Let's go," said Oscar as the group approached the door.

This is where Ishy stepped forward and put his computer geekiness to work. He had spent all day looking up different ways to pick locks via different websites and video tutorials. After watching every tutorial known to man he was convinced he could easily pick a lock using his pen, and he did just that: in a matter of seconds. Oscar had to admit, it was rather impressive.

"Ta-da!" he bragged as the door swung open.

This all seemed a bit too easy and too good to be true, but the others certainly weren't going to complain.

Oscar turned on his torch as the gang gingerly crept into the shop. Ishy stupidly slammed the door behind them which made the others jump.

"Ishy!" snapped Emma.

"Oh yeah, sorry," Ishy replied.

After a few angry glares towards Ishy, the friends slowly made their way through the shop. There was still an unpleasant stench but certainly not anything considered life-threatening.

They crept into the back room, where Miss Primrose kept all her stock. It was an unpleasant sight to say the least. There were jars of sugar coated toenails and toffee covered teeth. There were glass jars stuffed with snake skins, jars bursting with rotten eggs, candy floss that looked more like the hair of the elderly. Everywhere they looked there were containers brimming with the most repulsive 'sweets' you can imagine, and there were plenty of worms in jars – worms everywhere.

"I think I'm going to be sick," said Ishy as he took in all the disgusting sights.

"Just what is she up to?" Emma muttered.

Suddenly from the top of the shelves, Miss Primrose's cat leapt down and started to stare down the four friends. The cat's fur puffed up on its back and it began to hiss and the kids started to slowly back away.

"Someone give it a treat!" cried Reece.

"Don't be silly. Even the cat knows not to eat any treats from this place!" replied Emma.

The cat began to cough, almost as if it was struggling to breathe. But most shocking of all was the voice that appeared to come from the cat's mouth. "Ugh! Hair ball! Yuck!" The cat gagged.

"Okay guys, just so we're all clear and all on the same page – the cat just spoke, right?" muttered Reece.

The others didn't respond. They didn't have to; their faces showed their utter shock.

"Thought so," added Reece.

"Did you just talk?" Oscar asked.

"Sorry, I know I should have more manners but you have no idea how uncomfortable these things are," the cat said.

"What is going on?" Emma muttered in panic.

"Don't you recognise your favourite shopkeeper?" the cat asked.

"Mr McNulty, is that you?" Oscar moved closer to the cat.

"Yes."

10

"YOU'RE A CAT!" CRIED ISHY.

"Well spotted, old chum! I was wondering what all this fur was," replied Mr McNulty.

"I think what Ishy is trying to get at is…why are you a cat?" Emma asked politely.

"She's a witch!" shouted Mr McNulty. "She did this to me. She wanted to buy my shop from me – I told her it's not for sale and the next thing I know, she turned me into a cat!"

"I knew something wasn't right about her!" said Oscar.

"You have to stop her! She hates children! She wants to take over every sweet shop in the world! I can't stand it. When I saw her try and force that frog's eye down dear Emma, I had to intervene, I had to do something!" explained Mr McNulty.

"You stopped her from making me eat it," Emma said with a smile.

"But why does she want to take over all the sweet shops?" asked Reece.

"She blames sweets and sugar for children being happy, for children laughing, for children dancing, for children playing and everything. She won't rest until every child in the world is miserable, quiet, only speaks when spoken to and does exactly what they're told," explained Mr McNulty. "I fear what's next in her plan."

"That monster," Ishy said as he wiped a tear from his face.

"How do we stop her?" asked Oscar.

"Go to your parents or to the head teacher. We all need to come up with a plan to stop her," said Mr McNulty.

"I can't see our parents buying the whole witch thing," Reece muttered.

"Well, we have to try. The adults will be the only ones who know how to get rid of a witch," explained Oscar.

"I suppose they have their uses," Ishy sighed.

"Make haste, kids! We need to stop her! Quickly! I do have only two more lives in me after all!" sobbed Mr McNulty.

"Two? What happened to the other seven?" Emma asked in alarm.

"Well, the first time, I was so shocked to see myself as a cat, I ran off in a panic and was run over by Mr Mullan's ice cream van.

"The second time I tried to jump on Miss Primrose and scratch her for turning me into a cat, but she threw me out of the window and I fell head first onto the road.

"Thirdly, straight after my second death, I woke up where I'd landed and was run over by that blasted ice cream van again! So I was three lives down within my first few minutes of feline life.

"The fourth time I was trying to find something edible in this shop when I noticed some bacon on the floor. I couldn't believe my luck! I soon realised it was Miss Primrose's trap to catch mice and rats. The bacon was completely covered in rat poison. So after being sick many times, I soon slipped away.

"Fifth time I was put in Miss Primrose's washing machine and spun around for her entertainment.

"The sixth time I went to the police station – hoping someone would notice me, as I am a talking cat after all!

But I ended up getting sat on by a very fat policeman, and what a way to go that was! As for the last time – well I probably shouldn't say."

"Oh no. Go on. Tell us?" said Reece.

"Well let's just say it wasn't a very pleasant experience being three feet away from an exploding REEKFEST 4000," Mr McNulty said reluctantly.

"Oh yeah, sorry about that," said Oscar, rather embarrassed.

Reece turned his attention to Emma. "Never underestimate the power of the REEKFEST 4000," he said as Emma rolled her eyes.

"Anyway you've got no more time to lose! I'll be here keeping an eye on her. Go and get help," Mr McNulty said firmly.

"We've got to try and talk to our parents, guys. If anyone knows how to get rid of Miss Primrose I bet it's them!" said Oscar eagerly.

"Worth a shot," Ishy said.

Next would come the daunting task of trying to have a serious conversation about witches with their parents.

11

EMMA WALKED HOME FEELING sad. She lived at home with her dad but their relationship was a complicated one.

Her mother had died two years ago during a hostile attack on the overseas army base she was working in. Emma's relationship with her dad had struggled ever since. Emma's dad, Mr Baker, used the television in their house as an escape. He was constantly glued to his armchair with his huge headphones on, watching whatever – anything and everything: documentaries, news, sports, dramas, game shows… you name it, he watched it.

Emma was used to coming home from school to find her dinner – chicken nuggets, potato waffles and peas – waiting for her in the microwave.

This was all Mr Baker could ever bring himself to do. He loved Emma more than life itself but he was still nursing the broken heart he suffered when he lost his wife.

Emma knew this and accepted it. But deep down she felt she had also lost part of her dad the day she lost her mum. Sometimes late at night she would hear him crying from the pain he felt. She desperately wanted to run to

him and comfort him but she knew he didn't want her to see him like that.

Ever since her mother died, Emma felt she had also lost her home. Her house was still the same but everything that made it home had been missing the last two years. Emma's only release was music, she was gifted and often played beautiful pieces on the piano when she was sad. It gave her the power to express her emotions, she would love to play something for her dad but he was too busy losing himself in the television.

Sometimes, though, Emma still felt the presence of her mother whenever she was in bed feeling scared, lonely or distressed. She'd cast her eyes to the night-time sky, she'd see the stars strung across the velvety night and think of her mum. This caused the fear and sadness to disappear as if her mother's spirit was in bed comforting her with a cuddle.

Emma wished she could play music for her dad, she wished she could talk to him about her mother and just at this moment she wished she could talk to him about witches, but she knew it was no use. Mr Baker was incapable of believing.

12

OSCAR WASN'T HAVING any luck himself. It was hard to get through to his mum but for a very different reason. Oscar lived with his mum. His dad lived in Spain with his new wife and children, so Oscar very rarely saw him. Although his mum, Miss Nicola Tarrant, had originally taken the break-up hard, she'd become very passionate about fitness ever since.

Miss Tarrant was a bit ditzy but took enormous pride in her appearance. She was tall and slim with long blonde curly hair. She ran many fitness classes in the local area, including helping the elderly keep fit. If you know of anyone's granny that goes to Zumba classes, chances are they are instructed by Miss Tarrant.

When she wasn't running classes, she was on runs. When she wasn't running, she was at the gym. When she wasn't at the gym she was doing yoga, which is exactly what she was doing at home right now.

Oscar walked into the lounge where Miss Tarrant was already deep in her 'yoga zone'.

"Mum, can I speak to you a minute?" asked Oscar.

His mum was in the yoga position known as 'downward dog'.

She turned her head around slightly and rolled her eyes before taking deep breaths to regain concentration.

"Shouldn't you be in bed or doing homework or something? It's getting late now," she whispered.

"Mum, something really bad is happening and I need to talk to you," Oscar said firmly, desperately trying to get his mother's attention.

"We'll talk later sweetie," Miss Tarrant sighed.

Oscar knew there was nothing for it. If he was to have any chance of getting his mum's attention he knew he had to shout, so he cried out, "Mum there's a witch! A real life witch at Mr McNulty's sweet shop – she's serving kids horrible things and has even turned Mr McNulty into a cat!"

There was a brief moment of silence.

"Mum?" prompted Oscar.

"Sweetie, I can't have any of your negative vibes right now. It's affecting my energy flow," said Miss Tarrant.

"Mum, I need to talk!" Oscar shouted.

"Please be quiet sweetie. All you need to do is relax and breathe," Miss Tarrant said calmly before taking in a deep breath and shortly releasing it out.

"Silence isn't going to do anything Mum. I need to talk!" cried Oscar.

"Silence is not an absence it is a voluminous presence. Silence speaks with the voices of many and the voice of one. Unbroken, undisturbed, unknowing – silence is: perfection," quoted Miss Tarrant from one of her yoga tapes.

Oscar knew it was no use. He stormed his way out of the lounge, hoping one of the others was having more luck getting through to their parents.

13

"IT WAS USELESS," ISHY SAID, shortly after the gang met up the next morning in the playground. "The football was on last night. I've never seen the restaurant so busy! Beer and curry everywhere! My sisters were still cleaning up all the mess and sick when I woke up this morning, there was naan bread in the fish tank!"

"Any luck Reece?" Oscar said, hoping for some more positive news.

"Sadly not, guys. It's my parents' anniversary this week and they are doing all their stupid romantic things every day. Last night they had a candlelight dinner in the outer conservatory – it was disgusting," Reece explained, repulsed by the thought.

Just as Reece finished explaining, Emma arrived at school and joined them.

"Emma, please tell me you got some positive info out of your dad?" Oscar said with his fingers crossed.

"Erm well... I–" but before Emma could bring herself to think of an excuse, a familiar and terrifying sight once again appeared in the playground.

It was Miss Primrose. This time not only did Miss

Primrose have the megaphone but she also had a whistle around her neck. This she blew continually, until the children lined up in the playground. The kids knew to line up in silence, even the teachers in the school were lined up silently as they all stood to attention.

Miss Primrose smirked before raising the megaphone to her mouth. "*Silence*!" she yelled, even though the playground was about as silent as a playground could be. "I have an important announcement to make. After my meeting with Mr Fazey recently, we both agreed that the children at this school are a *disgrace*! *Hooligans!* Hooligans that must be disciplined. Therefore, as of this morning I am pleased to announce I am the new headmistress of the school!"

The pupils gasped, all too terrified to scream out in protest. The minds of eight hundred school children raced to deal with the news…

Where was Mr Fazey?

Something wasn't right.

Who is this woman?

What happened to that fat boy who was taken away yesterday?

Will we still get school dinners?

Nobody said a word!

Shock wasn't the emotion Oscar was feeling. He felt anger. His blood was boiling, his fists were clenched and clammy and they were shaking with his fury. Oscar couldn't stand it; he had to do something. "*She's a witch!*"

Oscar yelled. "She's put a spell on Mr McNulty and you can bet she's done the same to Mr Fazey!"

Some of the kids started chuckling. Most of them were still too scared to do anything, they all knew Miss Primrose was a horrible and terrifying lady but there was no way they were going to consider Oscar's crazy theory.

"Oscar, be quiet," Emma whispered.

"We know what you've done Miss Primrose! You're not going to win! You hear me! You won't win!" declared Oscar.

At that point it was almost as if Oscar had passed all his anger and rage on to Miss Primrose. Almost immediately it was her who started shaking, it was her clammy fists that were clenching and it was her face that looked about to burst.

"*You*!" she bellowed and there was no doubt she was pointing at Oscar this time. "My office, this instant!"

Oscar wasn't afraid of Miss Primrose any more, even though he knew full well what she was capable of.

14

"HOW DARE YOU!" Miss Primrose screamed as she slammed her hand against her desk. Oscar looked around the office. For someone who had only just become the headmistress, she had soon made the office her own. Oscar had been to Mr Fazey's office a couple of times before and the transformation was quite extraordinary.

Previously the room had been a shrine to education and Elvis – well mainly Elvis, there had been a velvet portrait of 'the king' above the headmaster's desk, replica white jumpsuit and a selection of memorabilia in a cabinet; there were some educational books in the corner. Now the room was dark, decorated in black, dark green and purple. There was black wallpaper, and horrible tatty purple curtains. Green folders and green books were stacked up in a horrible green bookcase, even the carpet looked unwelcoming, a vile dark purple colour that made your feet itch through your shoes. In front of the closed curtains there was an ugly black desk and chair.

"Who do you think you are?" cried Miss Primrose. "King of the gangsters no doubt. The godfather of the mafia. Well don't you worry, boy, your time will come.

You will be my warning, my example for all the other children who see you. Mark my words: boy."

"I know what you've done. I know you turned Mr McNulty into a cat and I know you've done exactly the same to Mr Fazey!" shouted Oscar.

Miss Primrose smirked and leaned forward onto her desk. "Prove it."

"You won't win. Somehow, some way we'll stop you," Oscar replied.

"I doubt that, boy. Who are people going to believe? The highly respected headmistress or a rowdy troublemaker like yourself, hmm? Or perhaps I should say thief! Imagine the trouble you and your friends will get into when they find out you broke into my shop! Ah yes, boy, I know all about that. I'll have you and all your little friends for that. Mark my words. Or perhaps I should let the police deal with you all? Breaking into lovely Miss Primrose's shop to steal her delicious sweets. They'll throw the key away on all of you! What in heaven's name would all your parents say? Imagine how disappointed they'd all be in knowing they raised a bunch of criminals."

Oscar was stuck. He wasn't sure what to say back.

Miss Primrose smirked before adding, "Luckily for you, boy, I'm just and fair. I'm willing to wipe the slate clean. As long as you show you're sorry, of course, we will then put this whole matter behind us. All you need to do is lines and have them on my desk by tomorrow."

Oscar rolled his eyes and sighed.

"The lines will say, 'I shall always respect my headmistress, she is just and fair.' This is to be written one million times by tomorrow morning."

"*What?*" Oscar shrieked.

"With this pencil." Miss Primrose revealed from her drawer one of the shortest pencils Oscar had ever seen, it was like a stump of a normal pencil.

"Are you serious?" Oscar examined the microscopic pencil.

"Deadly serious," Miss Primrose replied. "And don't try and cheat me, boy. This is a special pencil with unique lead. I shall know if you try to use another pencil."

Oscar sighed as he looked around the room. He soon noticed a fish tank on the other side of the bookshelf.

"Ah, I see you've noticed my little fish pets!" said

Miss Primrose. "You've reminded me it's their feeding time!" She walked over to the fish tank.

Oscar followed her to look closely into the dingy water. There were two goldfish frantically swimming around the tank.

Miss Primrose picked up a huge jar from a nearby purple shelf. To Oscar's disgust, as she buried her hand into the jar, he saw it was completely full of worms. She picked out a handful of wiggling worms before dropping them into the tank.

"I call these goldfish Fazey and Mikey." Miss Primrose simpered. "That little fat one's Mikey. He'll never complain about eating worms again."

15

"GOLDFISH?" CRIED EMMA, as Oscar regrouped with his friends after school.

"I'm telling you guys, both Mr Fazey and Mikey are now goldfish and being fed worms! We need to do something and do it now! We can't go another day with her at this school. Trust me."

"Emma, did you manage to talk to your dad?" asked Ishy.

"Erm, well not exactly," Emma muttered

"What do you mean?" asked Reece.

"I just couldn't get round to it. It's not easy bringing up the subject of witches y'know," Emma replied.

"Emma, we've got to go and see your dad right now and ask for help. He might be the last chance we have."

"I don't think that's a good idea," Emma said.

"It's the only way we can stop her!" cried Ishy.

"I said *no!*"

It wasn't like Emma to shout at the boys. They knew something was on her mind.

As the group cautiously walked past the sweet shop, they were taken aback by a piercing scream closely followed by a sharp cackle. The cackle undoubtedly belonged to Miss Primrose, it pierced you like ice and left you cold with fear. The gang was more worried about who her poor victim was. Even though Miss Primrose was now the new school headmistress, she still opened the sweet shop right on time for unsuspecting victims.

A girl in the lower years of the school ran out of the sweet shop sobbing her heart out. She was called Amy Johnson and was well known in the school for her long brown pigtails and gap toothed smile.

"What happened?" Oscar called out.

"W-w-well…sh-she…I-I-I asked for the white chocolate mice, then she gave them to me. I took a bite of one and it tasted funny…b-b-b-b-because it's a real dead mouse covered in white choc—" Amy sobbed before spewing up, right outside the sweet shop.

All the boys turned their attention to Emma; making direct eye contact with her.

Emma sighed. "Ugh, okay, we can try my dad but I promise you, it'll be a waste of time."

"Perhaps I could be of some assistance?" a voice enquired.

The gang looked down to see the feline version of Mr McNulty.

16

EMMA LED THE GANG back to her house straight away. As Emma expected the chicken nuggets and potato waffles were nestled in the microwave ready to be heated – she decided that dinner could wait.

The friends crept into the lounge and saw Emma's dad in his armchair with his headphones on as usual.

"Right where I left you," Emma sighed.

Mr Baker looked half asleep as he was watching the television. He seemed to be watching some bizarre program about clowns getting plastic surgery. The kids weren't convinced he was actually watching it; he looked brain dead.

"Ugh, Dad?" said Emma, but there was no response.

"Mr Baker?" Oscar said politely.

"*Dad*!" Emma shouted.

Mr Baker mumbled a little but certainly didn't give much of a formal response.

"Can I try something?" Ishy asked hesitantly.

"Sure." Emma shrugged, fighting back the tears at showing her friends how defeated her dad looked. It was breaking her heart.

Ishy approached Emma's dad, and stood behind his armchair. He then reached out and simply took the headphones off Mr Baker's head, hoping this might make a difference.

Mr Baker's expression didn't change: he didn't even blink.

"Dad?" Emma shouted again.

Mr Baker slowly turned his head towards Emma and her friends and murmured, "Yes, dear, dinner's in the microwave."

"It's not that," Emma said quickly before her dad thought to reach out for the headphones again. "I know it might sound crazy, Dad, but there's a witch at our school. First she took over the sweet shop and now she's the headmistress of our school! She's turned people into animals – including Mikey!"

Mr Baker sighed heavily. "Emma, these fantasy books you read have got stuck in your head. Maybe you should take a break from them. I got an email from your headmistress about Mikey – all the parents did. He's gone on a course to control his behaviour. And his bottom by the sounds of it," Mr Baker explained.

"Honestly Mr Baker, it really is true," stated Reece as Mr Baker reached for his headphones.

Suddenly a cat figure leapt onto the arm of Mr Baker's armchair.

"Perhaps you'll listen to me?" Mr McNulty said.

Mr Baker's face showed complete shock before he smirked and said, "Okay kids, very good! You almost got me, you really did. Come on then; which one of you is doing the cat voice?"

"They are nothing to do with it. I am Mr McNulty from the sweet shop and it's all completely true. Miss Primrose is a witch! She is the reason you see me in this state. I'm certain she has turned Mr Fazey and Mikey into goldfish, as the kids say."

Mr Baker went as white as a sheet. He had no idea how to react before muttering to himself, "It's official. I'm having a nervous breakdown. It's got to that point in my life where I've started to lose my mind."

"Dad, you're not going crazy! It's the truth. Miss Primrose is a witch and she won't stop till she has taken over every school and every sweet shop in the world. She hates children and wants to do everything in her power to make all the children miserable like her! Honestly, you have to believe us. You have to help us," Emma pleaded.

Mr Baker was still spaced out. His head was spinning. "She turned you into a cat…" he muttered, still trying to convince himself he wasn't going crazy.

"You need to help us," Oscar added to Emma's plea.

It was hard for Mr Baker to take in all this information. He had gone from watching a clown wanting to make their bum look bigger to tackling real life witches in a matter of minutes.

"Well if what you are saying is true," Mr Baker mumbled, still unsure whether this was some kind of incredible prank, "you have to soak her with water, so she melts."

"Of course! Like in the *Wizard of Oz*! Why didn't I think of that?" gasped Emma.

"Hate to burst everybody's bubble, but how are we

supposed to get away with soaking Miss Primrose in water?" questioned Ishy.

"You always have to spoil everything don't you?" Reece said to Ishy as he killed the buzz.

"You could always do it at night? I bet she'll be pottering about somewhere. I watched a program the other night about witches— witches are nocturnal," stated Mr Baker.

"That was badgers. It was a program about badgers," Emma corrected him.

"Oh well, yeah. That's what I meant," Mr Baker mumbled, embarrassed.

"We're going to get her at school," Oscar said. "I've got a plan. Mr Baker, could you help us?"

Mr Baker was still undecided whether or not this was some kind of clever joke the kids were playing on him. "I'm afraid my days of adventures and hunting witches are over. You kids have fun," Mr Baker said before placing the headphones back on his head and tuning back into the land of television.

Mr Baker was so wrapped up in his own grief that he couldn't bring himself to believe in any kind of magic, whether it be good or evil.

Emma's heart broke even more as her dad zoned back out. There was a time when Emma and her dad would have many adventures together. These ranged from searching for Big Foot in the forest, to getting hold of a map and hunting buried pirate treasure, to putting on their own puppet shows together for her mum. She wondered where that person had gone. She was desperate to get him back. But first there was a plan to put in place and a witch to exterminate.

17

THE NEXT DAY THE GANG met in the playground before school started. The plan involved the hose which was attached to the wall in the playground. Oscar, who hadn't done the lines Miss Primrose had demanded, was going to provoke Miss Primrose and lure her right on to an 'X' which Ishy had marked on the playground with white chalk. As soon as Miss Primrose was on the spot, the others would set the hose off and it would be goodbye to the wicked Miss Primrose. Well, that was the plan anyway.

"Easier said than done," Reece warned.

"It'll work. Trust me!" Oscar assured. "I think I know how to get to her and she'll chase me right to where we want her."

"Let's just get on with it! My nerves can't take much more of this!" cried Ishy.

"I'll go to her office now and bring her right here. Make sure you're ready," warned Oscar. He took in a deep breath.

"Just be careful," said Emma as Oscar nodded to her.

Everything was set up and ready to go. Now it was time for Oscar to once again visit Miss Primrose's office. Oscar's heart was beating rapidly. The walk to the headmistress's office seemed longer than ever before and Oscar's nerves grew by the second.

When he had reached the door his heart was beating in his mouth and a nervous sweat made his hands sweaty with fear. He reached out and slowly turned the doorknob before entering the office. The loud creaking of the door scared Oscar, shattering what little courage he had left; if he could have, he would have turned and run but the gang were relying on him, Mr McNulty was relying on him, the sweet loving children of the town were relying on him.

Before Oscar had even set one foot in the door, Miss Primrose barked, "So boy. Have you done your lines?"

"No," replied Oscar. "I'm not going to either…I am going to get all the teachers, and all the pupils in this school to believe me about you. We've got Mr McNulty with us and everyone is going to see what you've done to him. You can't win, Miss Primrose. There's nothing you can do to stop me!"

"*How dare you*!" Miss Primrose shrieked as she stood up from her desk. She took a step towards Oscar but as soon as she moved, he set off at a run with Miss Primrose close behind. The chase was on. Despite her wizened appearance Miss Primrose was fast, far faster than Oscar would have believed. Oscar was the fastest on his football team but she gained on him and with every passing second his lead was disappearing. Running through the hallway and screeching past the the staffroom Oscar pelted through the doors and back into the playground. Primrose was getting closer and closer by the second, and

Oscar could hear her grunting louder and louder as she got within an arm's reach.

As Oscar hurtled into the playground the children watched in shock as their new headmistress tried to set a new Olympic record with Oscar as the prize. Realising he had their attention, he started shouting as he headed for the 'X'.

"*Listen everyone!* I told you Miss Primrose was a witch and I'm going to prove it!" He ran past the 'X', just seconds away from Miss Primrose being right in position.

"You're finished!" Miss Primrose grunted, breathing heavily as she stood perfectly on the X, staring down at Oscar.

'*Now!*' Oscar screamed as Miss Primrose's attention turned towards the gang of friends and the hose that was pointed straight at her.

Emma turned the tap fast and hard. Nothing happened! She kept turning, a single lonely drip crawled out of the end of the hose and splashed pathetically on the playground floor.

The piercing sound of Miss Primrose cackling sliced its way through Oscar's soul.

18

"DO YOU HOOLIGANS REALLY THINK I am that stupid? You think I'd have running water here at my school?" Miss Primrose cried.

The gang's hearts sank. They were now at a complete loss – this was their last hope.

"I knew you would try a stunt like this. Which makes you *murderers*! Well let me tell you what we do with *murderers* at my school. We send them away for a very, very long time to a place where they swim all day and all night and only ever eat worms!"

Miss Primrose seemed to be getting taller and taller as she backed the friends into a corner. A bright red colour started to spiral in her eyes.

The friends started to feel weary as they fell deeper and deeper into a trance. It was clear Miss Primrose was putting a spell on them and they had no power to do anything about it.

Just before the spell had taken its toll, Mr McNulty's feline body flew up at Miss Primrose's face like a wild ball of teeth and fur, scratching and biting at Miss Primrose – he was a whirlwind of fury. This distraction broke the trance and the gang took cover behind a wall as brave Mr McNulty battled the evil Miss Primrose.

The friends watched in dismay as Miss Primrose threw Mr McNulty hard onto the playground and launched fire from her fingers into the brave cat that was once Mr McNulty. A fiery inferno hit him leaving a burnt lifeless corpse on the playground.

The playground gasped. They had seen Miss Primrose blast a cat to death. There was no longer any doubt: Miss Primrose was a witch!

"Mr McNulty!" Oscar screamed.

There was a sombre moment as they saw the smoking body lifeless on the ground. But they could only grieve for a second before Miss Primrose turned her attention back to the gang. Her scrawny figure seemed to swell as she addressed them in her moment of triumph, her voice had grown in power and our gang of friends couldn't help but shrink before it. She addressed the entire playground, her voice leaving their ears ringing with fear .

"This is only the beginning! Soon every school will follow my rules. Every child will respect my orders or spend the rest of their lives as a beast of my choosing! These four disgusting vermin will be prime examples! Being fish is too good for them. Watch how I transform them into worms to feed to the fish!" she cried with her piercing cackle.

She closed in on the gang once again as they ducked behind the wall, trying not to make eye contact. Miss Primrose closed the distance slowly, deliberately, each step bringing doom closer to the gang of friends.

However, with each step another noise grew – a distant siren was growing louder and louder by the second until a huge fire engine pulled up in the playground. Driving it was Reece's dad. He shot out of the truck closely followed by his wife, Mr Baker, Miss Tarrant and Mr and Mrs Kahn.

Reece's dad grabbed the hose from the fire truck and pointed it directly at Miss Primrose as she turned to face them.

"Give it up!" Reece's dad, Mr Goodman, called out.

Miss Primrose knew at this point there wasn't much she could do. She was either going to prison or going to be finished once and for all. If she was going down she was going to take Oscar and the gang with her. Her eyes turned bright red with anger, and fire crackled around her fingertips once more. As the flames licked around her wizened hands she screamed and began to launch magical fire at the friends. The second she moved she was met by a torrent of water as Mr Goodman released the hose and unleashed a jet of witch-melting water directly onto the evil Miss Primrose.

Her scream of anger suddenly turned into a scream of pain; a most disturbing sound. Her body shrank and melted away as the water soaked her from head to toe. Her body and clothes dissolved, leaving only green sludge on the playground floor. A foul burning smell emerged from the slime that had once been Miss Primrose and the children were disgusted. It was revolting; even worse than the REEKFEST 4000.

Before too long, Miss Primrose had completely vanished.

19

THE KIDS IN THE PLAYGROUND couldn't believe what they had witnessed. Admiring the slime that had once been their evil headmistress, a slow cheer filled the playground as the realisation dawned that Miss Primrose was no more. But the cheering was soon abandoned as the kids ran over to poor Mr McNulty's cat body.

They all had tears in their eyes; all except Ishy, who was crying like a baby.

"He saved us," Oscar croaked.

"Sacrificed himself for us!" cried Emma.

Suddenly, however, a white glow appeared from the cat's body and a huge white flash eclipsed the whole playground. To everyone's shock, Mr McNulty was now lying on the playground in human form.

He opened his eyes and began to cough. "You'd be surprised what you can live through," he said in a wheezy tone. "I did have one life left after all," he added with a wink.

The kids all gave Mr McNulty a huge hug. They were relieved. It didn't take too long for Mr McNulty to get back to his old self, soon asking if anyone knew what happened to his toupee.

Fortunately, the spell had also broken on Mr Fazey and Mikey, who transformed back into human form in the fish tank. Needless to say, the tank cracked and exploded with them inside it, but they were fine. It just took them a while to get used to walking again.

Emma ran over to her dad and gave him a huge hug.

"Emma, I'm so sorry I didn't listen to you. When you left for school this morning I kept thinking and thinking about what you said. I know you needed me and I haven't been there for you recently. But I'm here now, I promise. I spoke to your friends' parents and we knew we had to listen and do something. Your mum always told me no matter what happens I need to be there for you. I promise I will never fail you or her again. The truth is Emma, none of us has long on this Earth; life is fleeting. I promise from now on we are going to make every second count," said Mr Baker as he embraced Emma in a hug once more.

"You should have seen him, Emma! The way he got all the parents together! He was a real life hero," Miss Tarrant said as she kissed Mr Baker on the cheek.

"Eeeeewww Mum!" cried Oscar.

"I'm sorry too, sweetie," Miss Tarrant said to Oscar as she held her son tightly.

Ishy's mum and dad were making the most of the opportunity by handing out restaurant vouchers to all the kids in the playground. "Make sure you tell your parents it's two for one on Tuesdays!" Mr Kahn cried.

As for Reece's parents; well, Mrs Goodman was so impressed with Mr Goodman's heroic bravery she was too busy smooching the face off her husband to speak.

"Worst day ever…" Reece muttered to himself.

20

THINGS SLOWLY AND SURELY got back to normal. Mr McNulty was now back in his rightful place at the sweet shop. He got rid of the horrible tainted sweets Miss Primrose was serving and brought back all the sweets the kids loved. He also accepted life without a toupee and was very proud to sport his bald head.

Mr Fazey was back as head teacher at the school and his office was turned back into the Elvis shrine it had been before.

Unfortunately Mikey had actually become accustomed to eating worms. It took his parents a while to get him off them, but eventually he stopped. It did take him a while to set foot in a sweet shop again, but who can blame him really?

The kids were heroes. They were allowed free sweets from Mr McNulty's shop every Friday, which made Fridays even more delightful.

Emma had her dad back. He unplugged the telly and never got round to plugging it back in. TV was replaced by evening walks and a new adventure every day.

Shortly after the demise of Miss Primrose, Mr Baker

and Miss Tarrant started to date. This was a bit awkward for Oscar and Emma at first and led to a few jokes being thrown at them by Ishy and Reece, but they soon got over it. They were both pleased to see their parents happy and enjoying each other's company.

Ishy's parents' restaurant got even more popular! As soon as Mr Kahn introduced his latest dish, 'Chicken Primrose', people would travel from miles to try it.

As for Reece's parents, I'm pretty sure they are still smooching in the playground.

Mini – Marshmallows

GIANT
Strawberries

KEEP UP WITH THE AUTHOR

FOLLOW LAWRENCE ONLINE:

http://www.lawrenceprestidge.co.uk

Facebook:
https://www.facebook.com/LawrencePrestidge

Twitter: @LPrestidge7